The Forbidden Scroll

The Hidden Truth Behind Gay Love

Robert Joseph Greene

ICON EMPIRE PRESS

Toronto Vancouver New York
London

Robert Joseph Greene

Would You Mind?

Library of Congress Control Number 2013936890

ISBN 978-1-927124-29-1

Would You Mind?

CONTENTS

ACKNOWLEDGMENTS

I would like to thank: Bobby Nijjar, Tim Tewsley, Diane Bosman, Catherine Adamson for their support

1 INTRODUCTION:
MY FORBIDDEN WORDS

It is a known fact that you have to put more energy into protecting a lie than telling the truth. This Greek text was forbidden for the truth it revealed. 1800 years ago, Lucian of Samosata dared to show proof of how homosexual love might be equal (if not superior) to heterosexual love and the text has been suppressed ever since.

During the middle ages, monks purposely sought illiterate young men who they could train to copy images, in the form of letters. They were not able to read what they saw, because it was from the forbidden scroll.

In 1557, Pope Paul IV compiled and created the Index Librorum Prohibitorum (the Index of

Forbidden Books). The Index of Forbidden Books was a list of books all Christians were prohibited from reading or even owning except under special ecclesiastical permission. Ecclesiastical permission was rarely granted and those caught reading or owning these forbidden books would have been punished. Punishment ranged from ex-communication to a sentence of death.

What you are about to read is a fictional gay love story called "The Forbidden Scroll." The story is set around the discovery of the factual information found in "Amores" by Lucian of Samosata (the original forbidden scroll). The original unedited non-fiction translated text of Lucian's Amores will accompany the story so you can decide for yourself the truth.

Lucian of Samosata's works are part of the Index of Forbidden Books (Librorum Prohibitorum).

2 THE FORBIDDEN SCROLL

What words say ye?

News of the army had spread all over Summerset and our lot at the monastery was the last to know. Bishop Bertram was summoned to bring parchment and quill while we awaited the news. Soon we were to know our fate.

It was so said on parchment and then pricked to be copied. It arrived at half past. A crowd of scribes had formed at our bishop's arrival. Four scribes were assigned in haste to make copies. I was not one of them, for I, Terryn of Cole, aged fifteen years, was too young and too new to be trusted with such words. Besides, my skills were used only for translations, not royal news: Latin to text. Day in and day out, this was my fate.

To my father's demise, as second son, I received schooling but nothing else, only a place in the abbey as a scribe for translation. My brother, god rest his soul, was his heir, but is now gone and done in battle. He is no more.

Father said I was too soft and that a scribe's world is "sluggard's work". I disagree. The hand, as does this quill and parchment, eventually decays. I pray that forgiveness of my sins will flow freely when that time comes. Woe is me.

The work is harsh and grueling. Michael, the head scribe is merciless on mistakes. One scribe was banished for two days from the abbey without food, drink or shelter for just three mistakes on his work. A farmer took pity on him and he lived in a barn until his punishment expired.

But all has changed now. Our King has been defeated and we await our fate.

My eyes quickly scanned over the pricked parchment to find the name of our new King. We followed Bishop Bertram quickly for our lord does not step lightly and was needed post haste. The crowd was teeming with excitement and I had no opportunity to see when Alwin started his copy. So, I took a stool and sat watch over all.

As I peered from up high and over the shoulders of many, I caught sight of what I wanted to see.

King Cedric.

I saw that the clean parchment was sighted and blocked, which left very little room for copy.

Word spread around the kingdom like wildfire. A group of monks, mostly scribes, would be sent to the kingdom of Cedric up north to Deira, in Durham. We were there for their choosing.

That night I did not sleep well. I felt lucky that I was not a monk and therefore would stay, but what excitement if I were to be chosen. I was mixed in mind and heart at best.

The bells woke us for Morning prayer, but I was wayworn from lack of sleep. I donned my robe and fell step for the morning procession. I kneeled in queue and prayed in line. I spoke these words in prayer: "Forgive me, my lord, I still hath worrit my lord I reste my fate and the fate of my brethren in your hands, Amen."

When the prayers ended and we rose to get bread and wine, we heard the army approaching the courtyard. We were silent, but nerves pierced us far deeper than their arrows ever could.

We exited the abbey in solemn file and were brought before a knight and his army. We showed our submission to our new masters and bowed before them.

The air was brisk and we were shivering in the wind.

Sir Thomas, a tall, broad-shouldered warrior, and King Cedric's personal knight, dismounted from his heaving chestnut stallion and greeted our bishop who was kneeling before him.

"Rise and present your lot, Bishop Bertram," commanded the knight.

Our bishop then stood up and led the knight over to us and gave him our names and craft. "Alwin copies but does not read. Doran translates but does not copy." Gesturing towards me, he explained, "Terryn translates, copies, and reads."

The knight stopped and gazed upon me, for my robe was not the same as the others.

"Is he scholar or monk?"

"He is scholar my lord, but of noble breed," said the bishop.

This was all that was said and they moved on. "Leo, copies and reads. Josef, copies but does not read," and so on until all were presented.

The knight and the bishop walked back again, pulling most from line. I was one of them. My heart gasped and I felt faint.

"Collect your things, you will return with us," was all he said.
It would be a fortnight's journey.

The next day we set out north to our new kingdom to the North. We walked on foot carrying our possessions that fit neatly into our own blankets. After the day's walk, we were fed bread and ale. One Sundays we took time for prayer and received wine and boiled root vegetables as our special meal.

This went on for many days until we reached our new Kingdom. We were dispensed to wash. Instead of a abbey, we were sent to a monastery which already housed more scribes. Behind our immense hall lay an even larger castle, the likes of which I had never seen.

We lined up and knelt with hands clasped, on our knees with our heads bowed. Our robes were caked with dirt and sweat, and we were weary but glad that the journey was over.

Our new bishop was Bishop William of Durham. He was a plump man who seemed kind hearted. He let us rest before our assignments were given.

Days passed and routine set in. We ate, worked, prayed and slept in the one large hall in the monastery. There were long wooden tables, and when the dishes and utensils were cleared, the parchments and quills were presented. When at four and half past the hour, we were allowed a walk in the gardens before church service. It was then after the tables were cleared and we were bid to sleep on mats with stuffing.

The snoring and sounds were foreign to me. The guards walked afront and outside. Some slipped off to relieve themselves or drink without notice. As I tried to settle in, into my ears came a wailing sound. It was so faint that I could hardly trace the source. I convinced myself that surely I would not be beaten for leaving if I could lead all to the one in distress. So, I feigned sleep until the guards were distant, and then donned my robe to exit the great hall into the courtyard. Avoiding the patrols, I slipped into the castle.

The entranceway was dark and steep, and nary a soul seemed alive. The guards slept soundly in the inner chambers. However, the wailing became clearer so I followed blindly, not knowing my way about the castle.

I saw before me a large hall with large windows and a statue that lay at the foot of a grand stairway. At first dark, the clouds above cleared and the statue was struck by an eerie moonlight so as to make it clear and beautiful. On it was chiseled the words "King Cedric".

I climbed the grand stairs and found another set to the right. The sudden ceasing of the sound caused me to stop in my tracks. When it recommenced, I proceeded up the flight of narrow stairs. Now here the hallway was lit with oil lanterns and a guard was sleeping, unaware of my presence. The lamps burned brightly, illuminating many hanging tapestries of royal settings; and the floor was silenced with woven mats.

"The royal bedchambers," I thought to myself. "I will surely be beheaded for trespassing now," but the noise still drove me onwards.

I approached the door where the sound was loudest. I thought I would just peer in and speak not a word. The room was warm from the hearth to my right. It was a massive chamber, with a bed and lit lamp in the center. Sitting on the bed in a nightgown was the most charming boy.

I thought he would not notice me but I was wrong, because he stopped crying and looked right at me.

"Who are you?" he asked. "Speak."

"I am Terryn sir," I said, "a scribe. I heard a noise."

"I am Florian, prince of this estate. You are in my chambers," he growled most angrily.

"I am sorry my lord," I whispered as I bowed to leave.

"No wait, I won't tell, come here."

I obeyed. We were of the same age and height. His face was slightly scared but fine-boned. He noticed my inquisitive look.

He confessed, "I have a puss fever, and now one has a growth and I am in never-ending pain."

"Does it hurt now?"

"Yes, do you want to see it?"

My curiosity did vex me; I wished to know what ailed him.

So, he leaned forward and raised his gown to reveal his skinny nude body.

I saw nothing but angry red bedsores.

"Why there is no growth, just bedsores," I reassured. "Those are easy to cure. Just take vinegar and mint, and do not lie on your wounds." I explained that our old bishop had them and I was his chamber boy while he lay ill. During this time, I saw the doctor give him this remedy. I added that he needed to suck on lemons, too.

"I must go," I said.

"No, stay."

"I will get in trouble."

"How will I find you?" he asked.

"I am a scribe in the monastery, Terryn of Cole," I said as I slipped out and returned to bed without being seen.

Our Morning prayers took long here. Our new bishop used incense and more bells than we were use to at the abbey.

Clean parchments and old scrolls were placed before us and the room soon filled with the noises of work. I was translating into English a bundle of scrolled ancient battle reports of the Greeks from Thermopylae. King Cedric was back from the Holy Wars and his army had brought back thousands of tablets and scrolls in Latin, Greek and Aramaic which needed translation. Much work was needed to complete this enormous task. This is what they had pillaged the castles and churches for during the last conquest of Cole.

I was so immersed in my work that I did not notice when the room fell silent, but as the hairs raised on the back of my neck I sensed that there were people standing behind me.

"Might you be Terryn of Cole?" bellowed a low voice in the hushed room.

I swung around and to my surprise the king himself stood before me. I recognized him from the statue that lay at the foot of the grand staircase. I fell to my knees before my new king.

His gaze was horrifying to bear. I knew I was done for. With his hand on his sword, which rested on his hip, he tilted his head and reached over to see my parchment.

"Give it here."

I lifted the parchment, handed it to him while still keeping my head bowed.

He barely glanced at it before passing it onto a man that stood beside him.

"Is his work admirable?"

"Yes, your majesty it seems to be."

"Does he read?"

"Yes, your majesty, he does read."

"My son spoke of you giving him comfort. He said you gave sage advice on his infliction and he is doing better. But you are much needed here for we have few translators."

I said nothing but kept my head low.

"Tell my son that we cannot send him until evening," he said. Turning to me, he added, "You will be in my son's chambers at sunset and read to him."

I bowed my head lower in acknowledgment.

Later that day, a guard came and escorted me to the prince's chamber. I was surprised to see his tutor present, a youngish man who was tall, gaunt and seemed nervous.

The prince was out of bed pacing anxiously, waiting for my arrival.

"I have dried prunes, bread, wine and sweet meats for us," he said.

"What shall I read to you?" I asked. "I have nothing."

"Oh," said the prince, perplexed.

"Might I suggest, sire, we pick something from the library?" the tutor chimed in, ever so polite.

"Ah, a fantastic idea," said the prince.

So with great haste, we traveled down several corridors to a great room which housed rows upon row of books, so many that I could not count them all. The ceiling was high and it was cold and damp.

"Leave us," ordered Florian, much to the tutor's surprise. The tutor backed away without turning, gracefully bowing until he felt the door behind him and made his exit.

I was glad this was done for I was hoping for a moment alone again with the prince.

"Over there is a locked cupboard that I managed to pick open the other day, but the texts are all too odd for me to understand. I do not know this script. I know it is not Latin for I study it every day with my tutor. I was told you do translations. What think you of these?"

Walking over and unlatching the cupboard, he pulled down a single scroll wrapped in a faded red silk cloth. Inside the silk was a scroll of the softest vellum and penned with the finest craftsmanship. It was most certainly a copy. But by whom was it made?

"Where did this come from?" I asked.

The prince explained that a visiting Dominican friar from Leuven had several scrolls. The bishop burned most of them when the friar grew ill and died suddenly from sheep's cough. This scroll was under his bed which the bishop never saw.

We rolled the scroll open on the nearest table. Dust filled the area around it.

The wording was Greek, but of a particular kind that I could barely translate it. It was a dialect that I knew but rarely had the chance to see. At the top was written "Amores", with the words in Latin **librum prohibentur** written underneath.

"What does it say?" asked the prince.

"Amores forbidden scroll," I replied.

"Strange to have those words together, love and forbidden, do you not agree? Read it for me."

As I translated the words in my head, I saw words that were most evil and surely the work of the devil, but my eyes could not look away. I felt the devil within me. I was losing control.

"Terryn?"

He broke my trance.

"I cannot take the text but I wish you to read it," he begged.

I explained to him the nature of the text and why it was forbidden, expecting him to shy away and cringe at its vile context. However, Florian's eye became excited and he pressed for me to explain.

So I did, saying, "A Greek noble named Lycinus is reciting a great debate that he judged between Charicles, a man who loved only women, and Callicratides, a man who loved only men."

Florian's curiosity grew. "What say of it? We must make a copy...but how?"

"The scribes here cannot read, so call one to your chamber at night to copy. But be sure they are not from my tribe, for among us there are literates."

That night after we parted Prince Florian summoned a scribe to copy the text, and overnight it was completed. The prince returned the original to the library, taking care to lock the cupboard once the scroll was back in place.

All day my thoughts were on what forbidden words my eyes had seen, how my flesh had felt hot and uneasy and how I could not turn my thoughts away. I felt the devil had taken hold of me and I didn't want to fight. I wanted the day to end. My sinful curiosity filled me like a cup wanting of wine, not water.

Alas the day came to an end and we were cleaning our space for prayer and sleep. I was free to walk without a guard to the prince's private quarters. There, laid before us, were the newly copied parchments that would seal our fate.

Again, Florian had a spread of wines, sweets and meats for us to enjoy, a feast that I had long forgotten from my childhood manor when I lived with my family. Oh, how I missed the simple pleasures of noble life. Prince Florian also brought winter flowers and burnt sage for effect. It was such a kind and undeserving effort for me, his humble servant. I was speechless.

"I am truly happy for you brought me from death and boredom. You are kind beyond words. I shall repay you someday," I said excitedly.

Prince Florian was just as excited as I and wondered what the text would bring.

So I started to read...

"He (Charicles) rubbed his brow lightly with his hand and after a short pause began as follows: "To you, Aphrodite, my queen, do my prayers appeal to give help in my advocacy of your cause. For every enterprise attains complete perfection if you shed on it but the faintest degree of the arts of persuasion that are your very own; but discourses on love have particular need of you. For you are their only true mother. Come, you who are the most feminine of all, plead the cause of womankind, and of your grace allow men to remain male, as they were born to be. Therefore do I at the very outset of my discourse call as witness to back my plea the first mother and earliest root of every creature, that sacred origin of all things, I mean, who in the beginning established earth, air, fire and water, the elements of the universe, and, by blending these with each other, brought to life everything that has breath. Knowing that we are something created from perishable matter and that the life-time assigned each of us by fate is but short, she contrived that the death of one thing should be the birth of another and meted out fresh births to compensate for what dies, so that by replacing one another we live for ever. But, since it was impossible for anything to be born from but a single source, she devised in each species two types. For she allowed males as their peculiar privilege to ejaculate semen, and made females to be a vessel as it were for

THE RECEPTION OF SEED, AND, IMBUING BOTH SEXES
WITH A COMMON DESIRE, SHE LINKED THEM TO EACH
OTHER, ORDAINING AS A SACRED LAW OF NECESSITY
THAT EACH SHOULD RETAIN ITS OWN NATURE AND
THAT NEITHER SHOULD THE FEMALE GROW
UNNATURALLY MASCULINE NOR THE MALE BE
UNBECOMINGLY SOFT. FOR THIS REASON THE
INTERCOURSE OF MEN WITH WOMEN HAS TILL THIS
DAY PRESERVED THE LIFE OF MEN BY AN UNDYING
SUCCESSION, AND NO MAN CAN BOAST HE IS THE SON
ONLY OF A MAN; NO, PEOPLE PAY EQUAL HOMAGE TO
THEIR MOTHER AND TO THEIR FATHER, AND ALL
HONOURS ARE STILL RETAINED EQUALLY BY THESE
TWO REVERED NAMES.

As I read and shared in translation, my eyes
watered and my ears burned. The descriptions,
the words, were blasphemous and strange. They
revealed acts both lucid and vile. I could not
contain my excitement, nor could the Prince.

I continued:

BUT AT THIS POINT DISCIPLES OF SOCRATES CAN
RESURRECT THAT WONDERFUL ARGUMENT BY WHICH
BOYS' EARS AS YET INCAPABLE OF PERFECT LOGIC
ARE DECEIVED, THOUGH THOSE WHOSE MINDS HAVE
ALREADY REACHED THEIR FULL POWERS WOULD NOT
BE LED ASTRAY BY THEM. FOR THEY AFFECT A LOVE
FOR THE SOUL AND, BEING ASHAMED TO PAY COURT

TO BODILY BEAUTY, CALL THEMSELVES LOVERS OF
VIRTUE. THIS OFTEN TEMPTS ME TO CACKLE WITH
LAUGHTER. FOR WHAT IS WRONG WITH YOU, GRAVE
PHILOSOPHERS, THAT YOU DISMISS WITH SCORN
WHAT HAS NOW LONG GIVEN PROOF OF ITS QUALITY,
AND HAS WITNESSES TO ITS VIRTUE IN ITS BECOMING
GREY HAIRS AND ITS OLD AGE, WHEREAS ALL YOUR
WISE LOVE IS CAPTIVATED BY THE YOUNG THOUGH
THEIR REASONINGS CANNOT YET DECIDE TO WHAT
COURSE THEY WILL TURN? OR IS THERE A LAW THAT
ALL UGLINESS SHOULD BE THOUGHT GUILTY OF
VICIOUSNESS BUT THAT THE HANDSOME SHOULD
AUTOMATICALLY BE PRAISED AS GOOD? BUT INDEED,
TO QUOTE HOMER, THE GREAT PROPHET OF TRUTH,

ALTHOUGH ONE MAN IS WORSE IN LOOKS,
HIS FRAME GOD CROWNS WITH SPEECH, AND MEN
REJOICE
TO LOOK AT HIM. UNERRING DOES HE SPEAK
WITH CHARMING MODESTY, PRE-EMINENT
AMID THE ASSEMBLED MEN; WHEN THROUGH THE
TOWN
HE WALKS, MEN LOOK AT HIM AS 'TWERE A GOD.'
AND AGAIN THE POET HAS SPOKEN WITH THESE
WORDS:
'YOU DID NOT THEN HAVE WITS TO ADD TO LOOKS.'

INDEED WISE ODYSSEUS IS PRAISED MORE THAN
HANDSOME NIREUS.

Florian asked that I continued some more but I
was too weak. I had read and translated what
sinful words were before me but was confused by

the logic. I did not know if the forbidden text
cursed me because it gave me doubt in all things
I thought to be known and wise.

Before, I had thought that all was special between
man and woman to be true. Why would such be
questioned? Florian stammered in annoyance
that I had not shared what I just translated. I
relayed it word for word and explained it as devils
speak. I would not have believed it if I had not
witnessed with my own eyes. Florian was
unmoved and did not stop me from speaking. I
was greatly disturbed and tired from what I had
just read. I would have gone back to my
chambers had Florian not requested that I lay
with him.

I quickly feel asleep. As some point in the night I
woke and Prince Florian was nowhere to be
found. I looked and saw him on the balcony
across the room. The night clouds appeared and
disappear like the night before in front of the
statue. The moonlight gave Prince Florian the
most beautiful glow that I could not help but go to
him.

He was staring at the sky. I looked up as well.
The stars were out in brilliant glory. We stood
together, staring out at the night sky.

"The stars lead us to heaven," said Prince Florian, "So I shall pick one to protect us from our mortal sins, dear Terryn."

With that he took my hand and raised it towards the sky to a star that was not among a cluster but stood alone. The star was not bright but still noticeable.

"This is our star my sweet Terryn of Cole."

Still holding my hand, he turned to face me and drew me close to him. The warmth of his body in the cold night air was most welcome. A strange feeling came upon me.

"Kiss me," he said in a soft commanding voice, and he led me back to his bedchamber.

During the night, he indulged with me in the curiosities of the flesh. Desires that I dared not request of him or speak of came upon me like the forbidden fruit from Eden's tree of knowledge. Florian laid kisses upon my face until I was aroused, and then thrilled me with pleasures of ecstasy until we fell together in exhaustive discharge, of which I had known of before but only in private. Such sin rocked my very essence, but to my surprise had not bothered me, and I was able to sleep in Florian's arms.

However, guilt crept in like a black cat upon it's prey. I woke with such guilt and feelings of shame. My wretched body was not mine but owned by the devil. I left Prince Florian still asleep in his bed. Before the ringing of the bells of prayer I left to return to the monastery.

If I was not to be burned to stake for what sin I had done that night, I would then sure go mad with guilt. I had a mortal hatred within me for this weakness of my soul. My flesh burned hot from the devil's hand.

I walked outside in the freezing cold and felt no release from the fire that was within me. Although it poured rain, I felt no relief. Though wet from rain and sweat, I stopped and kneeled in the mud in agony. I prayed to God for forgiveness. Tears streamed from my eyes. I knew I had done wrong against our lord God though I could not blame Prince Florian, for I was sure the devil's hand had touch him too. I was sure the curse came from the forbidden scroll to both of us.

But, then it came upon me like a blessing. As if God spoke to me in prayer.

"A maiden shall be my savior."

I felt God's hand guide me as the rain washed me of my sin. The love of a woman will set me right. I thanked God for his wisdom. I thought best to share what God had shown me with Prince Florian.

As I entered the Monastery a pitiful mess, all who saw looked upon me in horror. Wet, weary, and tired, I went to my spot for Morning prayer. Though I had just prayed, I knew God wanted me to give thanks again to his honor before the bishop and among my brethren.

The day waned and I was wanting sleep, for the night past I had very little. I performed my translation duties with little desire. In time, my guilt gave way to desire again. I was told the devil has power most as the night approaches. Admittedly, I completed my duties in haste, for I longed to see more from the forbidden scroll. My thoughts drifted to Prince Florian and how kind he had been to me but our sin was unspeakable. How confused I was from the words I had read and the sins I had indulged in with the prince. I was truly vexed with confusion and still untouched by a woman's hand. I wanted to re-align myself towards goodness and remove all sin that has rotted my soul.

That night, I came to Florian ready to bare to him my soul and free myself from my guilt that has weigh upon me so heavily. I wanted to tell him that God had spoken to me in prayer and showed me the path for redemption for the both of us.

However, when my eyes came upon him, I grew weak with desire. I tried to speak but Prince Florian requested that I share these words later, for he wanted more from the forbidden scroll.

"We are at a crucial point you and I, and I want to read about what we have done, just as in the debate."

So, I read on.

TO QUIT THIS HIGHLY SERIOUS PLANE AND DESCEND SOMEWHAT TO YOUR LEVEL OF PLEASURE, CALLICRATIDAS, I SHALL SHOW THAT THE SERVICES RENDERED BY A WOMAN ARE FAR SUPERIOR TO THOSE OF A BOY. IN THE FIRST PLACE I CONSIDER THAT ALL KINDS OF ENJOYMENT GIVE GREATER DELIGHT IF OF LONGER DURATION. FOR SWIFT PLEASURE FLITS BY AND IS GONE BEFORE WE CAN RECOGNIZE IT, BUT DELIGHTS ARE ENHANCED BY BEING PROLONGED. HOW I WISH THAT STINGY FATE HAD ALLOTTED US LONG TERMS OF LIFE AND IT CONSISTED ENTIRELY OF UNBROKEN GOOD HEALTH WITH NO GRIEF PREYING ON OUR MINDS. FOR THEN WE SHOULD SPEND ALL OUR DAYS IN FEASTING AND

HOLIDAY. BUT, SINCE ENVIOUS FORTUNE HAS
GRUDGED US THESE GREATER BENEFITS, AMONGST
THOSE THAT WE HAVE THE SWEETEST ARE THOSE
THAT LAST. THUS FROM MAIDENHOOD TO MIDDLE
AGE, BEFORE THE TIME WHEN THE LAST WRINKLES OF
OLD AGE FINALLY SPREAD OVER HER FACE, A WOMAN
IS A PLEASANT ARMFUL FOR A MAN TO EMBRACE,
AND, EVEN IF THE BEAUTY OF HER PRIME IS PAST,
YET

"WITH WISER TONGUE
EXPERIENCE DOTH SPEAK THAN CAN THE YOUNG."

 BUT THE VERY MAN WHO SHOULD MAKE ATTEMPTS
ON A BOY OF TWENTY SEEMS TO ME TO BE
UNNATURALLY LUSTFUL AND PURSUING AN
EQUIVOCAL LOVE. FOR THEN THE LIMBS, BEING LARGE
AND MANLY, ARE HARD, THE CHINS THAT ONCE WERE
SOFT ARE ROUGH AND COVERED WITH BRISTLES, AND
THE WELL-DEVELOPED THIGHS ARE AS IT WERE
SULLIED WITH HAIRS. AND AS FOR THE PARTS LESS
VISIBLE THAN THESE, I LEAVE KNOWLEDGE OF THEM
TO YOU WHO HAVE TRIED THEM! BUT EVER DOES HER
ATTRACTIVE SKIN GIVE RADIANCE TO EVERY PART OF
A WOMAN AND HER LUXURIANT RINGLETS OF HAIR,
HANGING DOWN FROM HER HEAD, BLOOM WITH A
DUSKY BEAUTY THAT RIVALS THE HYACINTHS, SOME
OF THEM STREAMING OVER HER BACK TO GRACE HER
SHOULDERS, AND OTHERS OVER HER EARS AND
TEMPLES CURLIER BY FAR THAN THE CELERY IN THE
MEADOW. BUT THE REST OF HER PERSON HAS NOT A
HAIR GROWING ON IT AND SHINES MORE PELLUCIDLY
THAN AMBER, TO QUOTE THE PROVERB, OR SIDONIAN
CRYSTAL."

"Go on, we have not heard his reply," said the prince.

So I read and translated:

I THOUGHT THAT OUR MERRY CONTEST HAD GONE AS FAR AS JEST ALLOWED BUT, SINCE CHARICLES IN HIS DISCOURSE HAS BEEN MINDED ALSO TO WAX PHILOSOPHICAL ON BEHALF OF WOMEN, I HAVE GLADLY SEIZED MY OPPORTUNITY ; FOR LOVE OF MALES, I SAY, IS THE ONLY ACTIVITY COMBINING BOTH PLEASURE AND VIRTUE. FOR I WOULD PRAY THAT NEAR US, IF IT WERE POSSIBLE, GREW THAT PLANE-TREE WHICH ONCE HEARD THE WORDS OF SOCRATES, A TREE MORE FORTUNATE THAN THE ACADEMY AND THE LYCEUM, THE TREE AGAINST WHICH PHAEDRUS LEANED, AS WE ARE TOLD BY THAT HOLY MAN ENDOWED WITH MORE GRACES THAN ANY OTHER. PERHAPS LIKE THE OAK AT DODONA, THAT SENT ITS SACRED VOICE BURSTING FORTH FROM ITS BRANCHES, THAT TREE ITSELF, STILL REMEMBERING THE BEAUTY OF PHAEDRUS, WOULD HAVE SPOKEN IN PRAISE OF LOVE OF BOYS. BUT THAT IS IMPOSSIBLE,

"FOR IN BETWEEN THERE LIES
MANY A SHADY MOUNTAIN AND THE ROARING SEA,"

AND WE ARE STRANGERS CUT OFF IN A FOREIGN LAND, AND CNIDUS GIVES CHARICLES THE ADVANTAGE. NEVERTHELESS WE SHALL NOT BE OVERCOME BY FEAR AND BETRAY THE TRUTH.

...FOR MARRIAGE IS A REMEDY INVENTED TO ENSURE
MAN'S NECESSARY PERPETUITY, BUT ONLY LOVE FOR
MALES IS A NOBLE DUTY ENJOINED BY A
PHILOSOPHIC SPIRIT. ANYTHING CULTIVATED FOR
AESTHETIC REASONS IN THE MIDST OF ABUNDANCE IS
ACCOMPANIED WITH GREATER HONOUR THAN THINGS
WHICH REQUIRE FOR THEIR EXISTENCE IMMEDIATE
NEED, AND BEAUTY IS IN EVERY WAY SUPERIOR TO
NECESSITY. THUS, AS LONG AS HUMAN LIFE
REMAINED UNSOPHISTICATED AND THE DAILY
STRUGGLE FOR EXISTENCE LEFT IT NO LEISURE FOR
IMPROVING ITSELF, MEN WERE CONTENT TO LIMIT
THEMSELVES TO BARE NECESSITIES, AND THE
URGENCY OF THEIR DAY DID NOT ALLOW THEM TO
DISCOVER THE PROPER WAY TO LIVE.

...DO NOT, THEREFORE, CHARICLES, HEAP TOGETHER
COURTESANS' TALES OF WANTON LIVING AND INSULT
OUR DIGNITY WITH UNVARNISHED LANGUAGE NOR
COUNT HEAVENLY LOVE AS AN INFANT, BUT LEARN
BETTER ABOUT SUCH THINGS THOUGH IT'S LATE IN
YOUR LIFE, AND NOW AT ANY RATE, SINCE YOU'VE
NEVER DONE SO BEFORE, REFLECT IN SPITE OF ALL
THAT LOVE IS A TWOFOLD GOD WHO DOES NOT WALK
IN BUT A SINGLE TRACK OR EXERT BUT A SINGLE
INFLUENCE TO EXCITE OUR SOULS; BUT THE ONE LOVE,
BECAUSE, I IMAGINE, HIS MENTALITY IS COMPLETELY
CHILDISH, AND NO REASON CAN GUIDE HIS
THOUGHTS, MUSTERS WITH GREAT FORCE IN THE
SOULS OF THE FOOLISH AND CONCERNS HIMSELF
MAINLY WITH YEARNINGS FOR WOMEN. THIS LOVE IS
THE COMPANION OF THE VIOLENCE THAT LASTS BUT A

DAY AND HE LEADS MEN WITH UNREASONING PRECIPITATION TO THEIR DESIRES. BUT THE OTHER LOVE IS THE ANCESTOR OF THE OGYGIAN AGE, A SIGHT VENERABLE TO BEHOLD AND HEDGED AROUND WITH SANCTITY, AND IS A DISPENSER OF TEMPERATE PASSIONS WHO SENDS HIS KINDLY BREATH INTO THE MINDS OF ALL. IF WE FIND THIS GOD PROPITIOUS TO US, WE MEET WITH A WELCOME PLEASURE WHICH IS BLENDED WITH VIRTUE. FOR IN TRUTH, AS THE TRAGIC POET SAYS, LOVE BLOWS IN TWO DIFFERENT WAYS, AND THE ONE NAME IS SHARED BY DIFFERING PASSIONS. FOR SHAME TOO IS A TWOFOLD GODDESS, WITH BOTH A BENEFICIAL AND A HARMFUL ROLE.

SHAME WHICH TO MEN DOTH MIGHTY HARM AND MIGHTY GOOD.
NOR YET ARE RIVALRIES OF BUT ONE SORT; TWO KINDS
ON EARTH THERE ARE; THE ONE A MAN OF SENSE WOULD PRAISE,
THE OTHER'S TO BE BLAMED; FOR DIFFERENT IS THEIR HEART.

...IF AT ANY RATE ONE WERE TO SEE WOMEN WHEN THEY RISE IN THE MORNING FROM LAST NIGHT'S BED, ONE WOULD THINK A WOMAN UGLIER THAN THOSE BEASTS WHOSE NAME IT IS INAUSPICIOUS TO MENTION EARLY IN THE DAY. THAT'S WHY THEY CLOSET THEMSELVES CAREFULLY AT HOME AND LET NO MAN SEE THEM. THEY'RE SURROUNDED BY OLD WOMEN AND A THRONG OF MAIDS AS UGLY AS THEMSELVES WHO DOCTOR THEIR ILL-FAVOURED

FACES WITH AN ASSORTMENT OF MEDICAMENTS. FOR
THEY DO NOT WASH OFF THE TORPOR OF SLEEP WITH
PURE CLEAN WATER AND APPLY THEMSELVES TO
SOME SERIOUS TASK. INSTEAD NUMEROUS
CONCOCTIONS OF SCENTED POWDERS ARE USED TO
BRIGHTEN UP THEIR UNATTRACTIVE COMPLEXIONS,
AND, AS THOUGH IN A PUBLIC PROCESSION, EACH
MAID IS ENTRUSTED WITH SOMETHING DIFFERENT,
WITH SILVER BASINS, EWERS, MIRRORS, AN ARRAY
OF BOXES REMINISCENT OF A CHEMIST'S SHOP, AND
JARS FULL OF MANY A MISCHIEF, IN WHICH SHE
MARSHALS DENTIFRICES AND CONTRIVANCES FOR
BLACKENING THE EYELIDS.

...WHO WOULD NOT FALL IN LOVE WITH SUCH A
YOUTH? WHOSE EYESIGHT COULD BE SO BLIND,
WHOSE MENTAL PROCESSES SO STUNTED? HOW
COULD ONE FAIL TO LOVE HIM WHO IS A HERMES IN
THE WRESTLING-SCHOOL, AN APOLLO WITH THE LYRE,
A HORSEMAN TO RIVAL CASTOR, AND ONE WHO
STRIVES AFTER THE VIRTUES OF THE GODS WITH A
MORTAL BODY? FOR MY PART, YE GODS OF HEAVEN,
I PRAY THAT IT MAY FOR EVER BE MY LOT IN LIFE TO
SIT OPPOSITE MY DEAR ONE AND HEAR CLOSE TO ME
HIS SWEET VOICE, TO GO OUT WHEN HE GOES OUT
AND SHARE EVERY ACTIVITY WITH HIM. AND SO A
LOVER MIGHT WELL PRAY THAT HIS CHERISHED ONE
SHOULD JOURNEY TO OLD AGE WITHOUT ANY
SORROW THROUGH A LIFE FREE FROM STUMBLING OR
SWERVING, WITHOUT HAVING EXPERIENCED AT ALL
ANY MALICIOUS SPITE OF FORTUNE. BUT, IF IN
ACCORDANCE WITH THE LAW GOVERNING THE HUMAN
BODY, ILLNESS SHOULD LAY ITS HAND ON HIM, I
SHALL AIL WITH HIM WHEN HE IS WEAK, AND, WHEN
HE PUTS OUT TO SEA THROUGH STORMY WAVES, I

SHALL SAIL WITH HIM. AND, SHOULD A VIOLENT
TYRANT BIND HIM IN CHAINS, I SHALL PUT THE SAME
FETTERS AROUND MYSELF. ALL WHO HATE HIM WILL
BE MY ENEMIES AND THOSE WELL DISPOSED TO HIM
SHALL I HOLD DEAR. SHOULD I SEE BANDITS OR
FOEMEN RUSHING UPON HIM, I WOULD ARM MYSELF
EVEN BEYOND MY STRENGTH, AND IF HE DIES, I
SHALL NOT BEAR TO LIVE. I SHALL GIVE FINAL
INSTRUCTIONS TO THOSE I LOVE NEXT BEST AFTER
HIM TO PILE UP A COMMON TOMB FOR BOTH OF US,
TO UNITE MY BONES WITH HIS AND NOT TO KEEP
EVEN OUR DUMB ASHES APART FROM EACH OTHER.

There I stopped because guilt had crept into me
again. I placed upon him my heavy heart and
woeful burdens. I told him about God's path for
righteousness and redemption. Prince Florian
grew quiet and somber for he felt differently. His
heart wanted to be with me like man would be
with woman. If he could spare some gold coins, I
told him I would find us maidens to free us from
the devil's clasp.

"You shall go that path alone Terryn. Go get a
milk maiden, take some gold and show her." With
tears in his eyes, the prince reached into his floor
chest and presented me with golden coins.

"See her love for what it's worth. I shall lie here and cry because i know now that I need no other but you, my Terryn of Cole."

I was beside myself with sadness as I left the prince's chambers. "I am most wicked," I thought to myself, but I was sure God's guidance was the truth. I still heard his cries while I lay in the hall, and could not bring myself to sleep. How wretched a man was I.

The following day, I was a man on a quest. The guards knew all the wayward wenches well and so I consulted them for such information. I was advised to journey to Hogarth's Inn to find a willing hen and no gammer. After an hour's walk I found it to be an appalling place with the smells and sounds of unheard sins. There was gambling afoot and a bawdy house in back. I had heard of this place in words but never by sight, nor stench.

The innkeeper gave thought to my request and pointed towards a plumpish wench named Rose who sat among men with ale and laughter.

"I seek comfort," I uttered as I approached her.

"Ah, a monk or lass or stag?" she asked as her friends laughed at me.

"Stag with reward," I replied, revealing the gold.

All went silent as they stared in awe at the coins. I held the coins before her but not long enough for her to count them.

She smiled and motioned me to follow her to the back where ragged cloth curtains hung strung up by ropes to cover a series of alcoves.

I heard the grunts and smelled filth, sin, and sex abound.

She pulled back a curtain to reveal a plain area with dirty mats on top of straw for comfort.

She guided me in pulling the curtain closed behind her. She guided me to lie down as she knelt beside me. Her plumpish hands stroked my cock till it was hard and firmly pulled me towards her.

She relaxed beside me and lifted her dress to reveal her swollen breasts and belly. She guided me on top of her.

My first try was too high and met with a soft yelp from her mouth. But she took my cock and by her hand guided it lower inside her. Her innards were warm and the fit was nice, I thought, as I thrust myself upon her until my release. It was over in a few minutes.

But no redemption came upon me and guilt stay within me but only twice as much.
I saw no joy in her face as she took payment. She asked for less than the sum I had upon me. I paid her the sum from the coins given to me by my sweet prince. Guilt rained upon me, both for my actions, and for Florian who needed no proof. I was a fool. Florian had my heart not the devil.

That night I returned to him to apologize. A gift of fine woven clothes with vibrant colors awaited me on his bed upon arrival. They were so beautiful that I put them on at once. I was forgiven and love united us again.

"We must know the end of the story. I am certain it is our love that wins," said the prince.

So, I smiled and read and translated from the parchment once again:

...THIS TOO IS THE CASE GENERALLY. FOR, WHEN THE HONOURABLE LOVE INBRED IN US FROM CHILDHOOD MATURES TO THE MANLY AGE THAT IS NOW CAPABLE OF REASON, THE OBJECT OF OUR LONGSTANDING AFFECTION GIVES LOVE IN RETURN AND IT'S DIFFICULT TO DETECT WHICH IS THE LOVER OF WHICH, SINCE THE IMAGE OF THE LOVER'S TENDERNESS HAS BEEN

REFLECTED FROM THE LOVED ONE AS THOUGH FROM
A MIRROR. WHY THEN DO YOU CENSURE THIS AS
BEING AN EXOTIC INDULGENCE OF OUR TIMES,
THOUGH IT IS AN ORDINANCE ENACTED BY DIVINE
LAWS AND A HERITAGE THAT HAS COME DOWN TO
US? WE HAVE BEEN GLAD TO RECEIVE IT AND WE
TEND ITS SHRINE WITH A PURE HEART. FOR THAT
MAN IS TRULY BLESSED ACCORDING TO THE VERDICT
OF THE WISE,

"WHOSO HATH YOUTHFUL LADS AND WHOLE-HOOVED
STEEDS;
AND THAT OLD MAN DOTH AGE WITH GREATEST EASE
WHOM YOUTHS DO LOVE."

THE TEACHING OF SOCRATES AND HIS FAMOUS
TRIBUNAL OF VIRTUE WERE HONOURED BY THE
DELPHIC TRIPOD, FOR THE PYTHIAN GOD UTTERED AN
ORACLE OF TRUTH,

"OF ALL MEN SOCRATES THE WISEST IS."

FOR ALONG WITH THE OTHER DISCOVERIES WITH
WHICH HE BENEFITED HUMAN LIFE DID HE NOT ALSO
WELCOME LOVE OF BOYS AS THE GREATEST OF
BOONS?
49. ONE SHOULD LOVE YOUTHS AS ALCIBIADES WAS
LOVED BY SOCRATES WHO SLEPT LIKE A FATHER WITH
HIM UNDER THE SAME CLOAK. AND FOR MY PART I
WOULD MOST GLADLY ADD TO THE END OF MY
DISCOURSE THE WORDS OF CALLIMACHUS AS A

MESSAGE TO ALL:

"MAY YOU WHO CAST YOUR LONGING EYES ON
YOUTHS
SO LOVE THE YOUNG AS ERCHIUS BID YOU DO,
THAT IN ITS MEN YOUR CITY MAY BE BLESSED."

KNOWING THIS, YOUNG MEN, BE TEMPERATE WHEN
YOU APPROACH VIRTUOUS BOYS. DO NOT FOR THE
SAKE OF A BRIEF PLEASURE SQUANDER LASTING
AFFECTION, NOR TILL YOU'VE REACHED MANHOOD
PUT ON SHOW COUNTERFEIT FEELINGS OF AFFECTION,
BUT WORSHIP HEAVENLY LOVE AND KEEP YOUR
EMOTIONS CONSTANT FROM BOYHOOD TO OLD AGE.
FOR THOSE WHO LOVE THUS, HAVING NOTHING
DISGRACEFUL ON THEIR CONSCIENCE, FIND THEIR
LIFETIME SWEETEST AND AFTER THEIR DEATH THEIR
GLORIOUS REPORT GOES OUT TO ALL MEN. IF IT'S
RIGHT TO BELIEVE THE CHILDREN OF PHILOSOPHY,
THE HEAVENS AWAIT MEN WITH THESE IDEALS AFTER
THEIR STAY ON EARTH. BY ENTERING A BETTER LIFE
AT DEATH THEY HAVE IMMORTALITY AS THE REWARD
FOR THEIR VIRTUE."

"So that is it. We won. By the call of virtue, our
love is most pure."

"Yes", I said, taking Florian into my arms.

I brought the forbidden scroll to his bed and read
the conclusion into his ear.

AFTER CALLICRATIDAS HAD DELIVERED THIS VERY
SPIRITED SERMON, CHARICLES TRIED TO SPEAK FOR A
SECOND TIME BUT I STOPPED HIM; FOR IT WAS NOW
TIME TO RETURN TO THE SHIP. THEY PRESSED ME TO
PRONOUNCE MY OPINION, BUT, AFTER WEIGHING UP
FOR A SHORT TIME THE SPEECHES OF BOTH, I SAID:
"YOUR WORDS, MY FRIENDS, DO NOT SEEM TO ME TO
HE HURRIED, THOUGHTLESS IMPROVISATIONS, BUT
GIVE CLEAR PROOF OF CONTINUED AND, BY HEAVEN,
CONCENTRATED THOUGHT. FOR OF ALL THE POSSIBLE
ARGUMENTS THERE'S HARDLY ONE YOU'VE LEFT FOR
ANOTHER TO USE. AND, THOUGH YOUR EXPERIENCE
OF THE WORLD IS GREAT, IT IS SURPASSED BY YOUR
ELOQUENCE, SO THAT I FOR ONE COULD WISH, IF IT
WERE POSSIBLE, TO BECOME THERAMENES, THE
TURNCOAT, SO THAT YOU COULD BOTH BE VICTORIOUS
AND WALK OFF ON EQUAL TERMS. HOWEVER, SINCE I
DO NOT THINK YOU'LL LET THE MATTER BE, AND I
MYSELF AM RESOLVED NOT TO BE EXERCISED ON THE
SAME TOPIC DURING THE VOYAGE, I SHALL GIVE THE
VERDICT THAT HAS STRUCK ME AS THE FAIREST.
MARRIAGE IS A BOON AND A BLESSING TO MEN WHEN
IT MEETS WITH GOOD FORTUNE, WHILE THE LOVE OF
BOYS, THAT PAYS COURT TO THE HALLOWED DUES OF
FRIENDSHIP, I CONSIDER TO BE THE PRIVILEGE ONLY
OF PHILOSOPHY. THEREFORE ALL MEN SHOULD
MARRY, BUT LET ONLY THE WISE BE PERMITTED TO
LOVE BOYS, FOR PERFECT VIRTUE GROWS LEAST OF
ALL AMONG WOMEN. AND YOU MUST NOT BE ANGRY,
CHARICLES, IF CORINTH YIELDS TO ATHENS."
AFTER GIVING THIS DECISION HURRIEDLY IN A FEW
BRIEF WORDS OUT OF REGARD FOR MY FRIEND, I

ROSE TO MY FEET. FOR I SAW THAT HE WAS UTTERLY
DEJECTED, ALMOST LIKE ONE CONDEMNED TO DEATH.
BUT THE ATHENIAN LEAPT UP JOYOUSLY WITH A
GLEEFUL EXPRESSION ON HIS FACE AND STARTED TO
STALK ABOUT IN FRONT OF US MOST TRIUMPHANTLY,
JUST AS IF, ONE WOULD HAVE THOUGHT, HE HAD
DEFEATED THE PERSIAN FLEET AT SALAMIS. I
DERIVED A FURTHER BENEFIT FROM MY VERDICT
WHEN HE ENTERTAINED US TO A MAGNIFICENT FEAST
TO CELEBRATE HIS VICTORY. FOR HIS BEHAVIOUR
HAD IN OTHER WAYS, TOO, SHOWN HIM TO BE
GENEROUS OF SPIRIT. AS FOR CHARICLES, I CONSOLED
HIM QUIETLY BY REPEATEDLY EXPRESSING MY
GREAT ADMIRATION FOR HIS ELOQUENCE AND HIS
ABLE DEFENCE OF THE MORE AWKWARD CAUSE.

That night our love making was tender. It was a
moment of truth beyond measure. We fell asleep
truly as one.

I was awoken with a splash of cold water which
jolted my nude body awake. Before me were 3
guards and the bishop, the forbidden parchment
in hand. Prince Florian and I lay there in bed,
frozen with fear.

We heard footsteps from behind. My heart
pounded as I sat up in bed, startled. "What in the
devil's name is going on here," demanded a
bellowing voice. It was the king. I looked at the
prince beside me, who was scurrying to find his
clothes beside the bed. Suddenly the room was

filled with even more people. There was chaos everywhere as I heard him yell, "Take him away! I need to deal with my son." Before I could digest what was happening, I was hauled to my feet and escorted outside by two of the guards.

Fear gripped me. What was to happen? What was to become of me? And more importantly, what would happen to my prince?

I was taken up through a back staircase of which I knew not before, rough hands pulling me every which way. I wanted to scream, to fight, but I knew I had no chance of struggling free. I prayed to god to have mercy on me. A door was opened in front of me, the hands pushing me into the middle of a room. Darkness enveloped me as the door slammed shut. Only a thin beam of light shined through the one window up high. The room was vile and rank most foul. I was locked in the towers.

Time seemed to blend into itself. Loneliness crept in and days seemed like weeks, weeks like months. I soon lost track of how long I had been imprisoned there. My hair had grown long. My own body was of the most foul odor. I used some of my drinking water for wash but not too much. With the few gold coins remaining that were given to me by the Prince. I was able to bribe the guard for fresh straw. The guard allowed me to clean out the sullen straw every so often.

Each night, what kept me sane, my only solace, was looking up to the nighttime stars to find the one my prince had chosen for us. I would then pray on that star that the lord would keep my prince safe, hoping my thoughts would somehow reach him. I no longer cared what would become of me and would have gladly taken the punishment for both of us.

One night, in what might have been the third month of my imprisonment, I was kneeling on the floor looking up at that window, praying to God for deliverance. The room was dark and cool for there was a new moon out, allowing a little light to shine into my cell. I imagined my prince, his hair rumpled and his dark brown eyes sparkling, the feel of his soft skin against mine. I could almost smell his breath on my face, hear the creaking of his door as he opened himself to me. I quickly realized that I was still sane and that the creaking was real. I snapped out of my dreamlike state and sat up, alert. The door seemed to take forever to open. Light streamed in from a torch in the hallway. I thought, "What new hell could God have in store for me? Was this my end?"

A dark figure stealthily entered the room. "Keep quiet," whispered a hushed voice. "Follow me, quickly." That voice. I knew that voice. Disbelief filled me to the core, and with it, I felt the first sense of hope I had since my imprisonment. I stepped forward and dared to remove the man's hood. I gently pulled it back, revealing the face of my beloved. However, what I sore shocked me. His face was swollen and bruised all over like he had been beaten unmercifully.

"My Lord!" I exclaimed, I fell to my knees and cried in joy.

"Get a hold of yourself," he said. "Yes, my Terryn of Cole. This is no dream, but we must go in haste. We only have a few minutes before the guards come back. Quickly, follow me."

With that we left, sneaking down the stair well and through the courtyard where a horse awaited us behind one of the outbuildings. As the horse took us to our freedom, I looked back on the place where I had found both love and terror, to the tower, the great hall, and to the castle that now housed no prince within.

I turned toward my prince and wrapped my arms around his chest, feeling his heart beating underneath his tunic. It was warm to my touch though the night was crisp and cold. Then, instinctively I looked up to the night sky, noticing a small twinkle of star which was the direction we followed in the otherwise black sky. Holding on tightly, I continued to stare upward and though as if we were following this great star in the sky…would it lead us to our freedom?

The End

3 NOTATION:
AMORES
by Lucian of Samosata
(referred to as Pseudo-Lucian):

Lycinus:

1. All day long, my dear Theomnestus, you've spoken of nothing but love and its games. Still I have not tired of listening to you pour out your joyful themes. I'd had an earful of serious matters, and thirsted for such diversion. The spirit does not suffer restraint gladly; it needs a bit of relaxation, a taste of pleasure. The whole morning your stories, as delightful as they are vivid, have so thrilled me that I felt like Aristides of Miletus, that enchanting spinner of bawdy yarns. I swear upon these loves, to which you have presented such a large target, I would resent it greatly were you not to tell me more! I beseech you - in the name of Aphrodite herself should you

think I am not serious - to draw from your memory another of your sweet adventures with this or that sex. Besides, today is Hercules' holiday, to whom we must sacrifice, and you are not unaware, I trust, of how much this god was captivated by the subject of Aphrodite; your tales will please him more than victims.

Theomnestus:
2. You could sooner, Lycinus, count the waves in the sea, or the rushing flakes of snow, than my many loves. I truly believe I have exhausted all their arrows so that, should they want to mount another attack, their unarmed hand will only draw laughter. Almost from the day my childhood gave way to youth I yielded myself to them to feast upon me. Loves followed thick upon each other - before one had ended another began; true Lernean heads, more numerous than that of the Hydra, and defying the flaming brands of Iolaus, as if fire could ever put out fire. Without a doubt there is a lodestone in my eyes that tirelessly draws all who are beautiful. I have even asked myself more than once whether so many favors were not some curse of Aphrodite. And yet I'm not a daughter of the Sun, nor an insolent Lemnian, nor some hypocritical Hippolytus.

Lycinus:
3. Spare me your hypocrisy, Theomnestus! What? You would blame Fortune for a life awash

in pretty women, and boys in the flower of their youth? Perhaps we should hold atonement sacrifices to cure you of such a dread disease. All kidding aside, consider yourself lucky that the gods did not fate you to the grimy toil of the farmer, the peregrinations of the merchant, or the dangers of army life. Your only care in the world is to stroll through the athletic fields, to primp the folds of your purple robe, or to do up your hair more artfully. Besides, these torments of love you gripe about only heap delight upon delight, and desire's bite is sweet. When you have set upon a conquest you know the joys of hope. When you are the victor you know those of enjoyment: the present and the future hold nought but delectation for you. Just now, as you were drawing up the tally of your loves with a precision worthy of a Hesiod, your eyes were bathed in joyous drunkenness, your voice flowed more sweetly than that of the daughter of Lycambes, and your whole demeanor shouted out that you were not left cold by the recollection of your delights. Therefore I beg of you, if you have neglected some little corner of your voyage with Aphrodite, repair the fault right away: Hercules will have his victim whole.

Theomnestus:
4. This god, Lycinus, is an eater of oxen. What's more, he likes his victims steaming. If we should

limit our offerings to stories, mine have dragged on long enough and will soon become tiresome. Your turn, please. Let your own Muse, casting off her usual gravity, chant us songs to put a pleasing end to our day with the god! There is a subject you have not broached, and which I would like to put to the test of your judgement: Which in your opinion is best: the love of boys, or that of women? I, who am smitten by both, lean neither this way nor that, but keep in balance the two arms of the scale. You who are not involved, give me your impartial opinion. Tell me frankly, o dear friend, which side you are on, now that I have told you of my loves.

Lycinus:

5. Do you imagine, Theomnestus, this is some kind of game? This is a matter requiring serious study. I myself have recently given it thought, and well do I know its complications, having been present at a heated debate between two friends whose words still ring in my ears. Their arguments reflected the opposition of their views, which was absolute. They did not enjoy this happy mean for which I congratulate you, and which lets you collect double pay, since you, sleepless shepherd, 'First guard the cattle, and then the sheep.' The first of these gentlemen found his delight in boys, and compared feminine

Aphrodite to the pit of doom; the second,
unstained by male love, was crazy about women.
They asked me to referee their battle of words,
and I can't tell you how much I enjoyed it. Their
arguments are engraved in my memory as if they
had just uttered them. I will try to recall them
faithfully, to give you some small proof of my
good will.

Theomnestus:
Allow me to shift my seat the better to see you,
'Waiting for Achilles to make an end of his song,'
and you, please give voice to the melodious glory
of this debate on love.

Lycinus:
6. Intending to head for Italy, I had a speedy
vessel readied, the kind of bireme used above all
by the Liburnians of the Ionian Gulf. After having
paid my respects to the gods of the fatherland,
and supplicated Zeus the Protector to look with
favor upon this lengthy expedition, I had the
mules saddled and headed for the shore. I said
my goodbyes to the men who had accompanied
me; they were gentlemen of wit and knowledge
who, after having sought my company, wanted to
convey their sadness at my leaving. Upon
boarding the vessel I took my seat at the stern
beside the helmsman. The oarsmen had already
rowed us offshore when the wind rose. Soon the

mast was stepped, the yard was run up and we made sail. The canvas filled, and we shot like an arrow over the foaming waves, noisily rent asunder by our plunging bow.

7. But the details of our voyage, interesting or not, are beside the point. After having followed the Cilician coast and having reached the Gulf of Pamphylia we passed, not without some trouble, the Swallow Islands, those happy boundaries of ancient Greece. Then we visited the main towns of Lycia, interesting more for their history than for their monuments, since they have retained none of their former splendor. Finally, upon reaching Rhodes, the City of the Sun God, we decided to take a break from our travels.

8. The ship was hauled out and the sailors pitched their tents nearby. As for me, having taken lodgings across from Bacchus' temple, I headed for it at my leisure, abandoning myself to a thousand impressions, one sweeter than the other. By its beauty, the City of the Sun God is indeed worthy of the name. Along the way I made the rounds of the portico in the temple of Bacchus, admiring the paintings that retrace the heroic fables and are as pleasing as they are instructive. At any rate, two or three guides had already taken charge of me and, in exchange for

a couple of obols, explained that which I had not understood or only suspected.

9. After having my fill of this spectacle I was getting ready to return to my lodgings when I had the most enjoyable surprise that a trip abroad can offer: that of meeting old friends, ones who are not unknown to you since you have run into them often at my house. One was Charícles of Corinth, a young man whose good looks are matched by his elegance, since he always wants to stand out to please the ladies. With him was Callicratídas, the Athenian, a man of the simplest appearance, as behooves one of our principal orators and lawyers. This latter besides is devoted to physical exercise, not so much for the love of the gym as for the love of the boys, a passion which totally transports him - he detests the fair sex to the point where he often curses Prometheus. As soon as they saw me, the two ran up, overjoyed; after the customary embraces each clasped me by the hand and insisted that I accept his hospitality. Seeing that their friendly rivalry was growing heated, I said, "Today, Callicratídas and Charícles, I will resolve your dispute by inviting you to my place. The following days, for I expect to stay here three or four, I will take turns being the guest of each of you, and we will draw lots to determine who will be first."

10. And so it was decided. That day they were my guests. The next day I was hosted by Callicratídas, and the following by Charícles. I discerned in the arrangements of each household the proof of their tastes. The Athenian was surrounded by beautiful boys. All his servants were beardless, and remained at his side only upon that condition. As soon as the least down shaded their cheeks they were sent to work his lands in Attica. Charícles, in comparison, was surrounded by a veritable orchestra of female dancers and musicians, and his house was filled with women as if at a feast of Demeter. You could not have found a single representative of the other sex, unless it was perhaps a little child or some old cook who, due to his age, could not inspire any jealousy. There you had, as I have said, clear indications of their respective inclinations. Often brief skirmishes broke out between them on this topic, but the issue was never settled. That is how things stood when the time came for me to continue my voyage. But this time I was no longer leaving alone: my two friends had decided to accompany me, wanting to visit Italy as well.

11. We could not pass up the chance to stop in Cnidus, where there is so much to be seen, notably the temple of Aphrodite which encloses the statue by Praxiteles, so admired for its beauty. We made a gentle landfall amid a

splendid calm, as if the goddess herself had propelled our vessel. After alighting, and while rooms were being arranged, I took the two experts on love by the arm and we went round Cnidus, delighting in the erotic terra cottas, worthy of a town dedicated to Aphrodite. After having seen the portico of Sostratos and a couple of other landmarks, we directed our steps towards the temple of the goddess, Charícles and I with the greatest satisfaction, but Callicratídas not without some reservations, as if this visit were an homage to a woman. He would have, I believe, willingly traded the Aphrodite of Cnidus for the Eros of Thespiae.

12. As soon as we reached the confines of the temple we felt as if caressed by the very breath of the goddess. The floor of the court had not been doomed to sterility by a stone pavement, but on the contrary, it burst with fertility, as behooves Aphrodite: fruit trees with verdant foliage rose to prodigious heights, their limbs weaving a lofty vault. The myrtle, beloved by the goddess, reached up its berry-laden branches no less than the other trees which so gracefully stretched out. They never know foliage grown old, their boughs always being thick with leaves. To tell the truth, you can notice among them some infertile trees, but they have beauty as their fruit. Such were the cypress and the planes which towered to the

heavens, as well as the tree of Daphnis, who once fled Aphrodite but now has come here to seek refuge. Ivies entwine themselves lovingly around each of these trees. Heavy clusters of grapes hang from the gnarled vines: indeed, Aphrodite is only more attractive when united with Bacchus; their pleasures are sweeter for being mixed together. Apart, they have less spice. Under the welcome shade of the boughs, comfortable beds await the celebrants - actually the better people of the town only rarely frequent these green halls, but the common crowds jostle there on festive days, to yield publicly to the joys of love.

13. When we had exhausted the charms of these places we pressed on into the temple itself. The goddess stands in the center; her statue made of marble from Paros. Her lips are slightly parted by a lofty smile. Nothing hides her beauty, which is entirely exposed, other than a furtive hand veiling her modesty. The art of the sculptor has succeeded so well that it seems the marble has shed its hardness to mold the grace of her limbs. Charícles, dazed by this spectacle, impulsively burst out, "Lucky Mars, to be chained by such a goddess!" He rushed forward as he spoke, lips pursed, neck stretched to give her a kiss. Callicratídas watched the display in silence. The temple has a second entrance for those who wish to contemplate the goddess from behind, for none

of her parts should escape admiration. It is easy in that fashion to gaze upon her hind beauty.

14. Wanting to see the goddess entire we approached this gate. Upon being let in by the woman who kept the keys, we were overwhelmed by her abundant beauty. As soon as the Athenian, who had so far been indifferent, glimpsed this side of the goddess, which reminded him of boys, he exclaimed with even greater enthusiasm than that of Charícles, "By Hercules, what a harmonious back. What rounded thighs, begging to be caressed with both hands! How well the lines of her cheeks flow, neither too skinny, showing the bones, nor so voluminous as to droop! How inexpressible the tenderness of that smile pressed into her dimpled loins! How precise that line running from thigh, to leg, to foot! Now I can understand why Zeus' nectar is so sweet when Ganymede pours it. As for me, I would never take it from Hebe's hand." While Callicratídas was declaiming this speech with much elan, Charícles remained fixed in place, the tenderness of his gaze betraying his emotions.

15. Filled with admiration, we noticed behind one of the thighs a stain like one on a robe, which only brought out the whiteness of the marble. It seemed a flaw in the stone. This kind of defect is

not uncommon, and fate thus tends to thwart that which otherwise would reach perfection. Supposing this dark stain was natural, my admiration for Praxiteles only increased, for having so skillfully hidden it where it would least be noticed. But the groundskeeper, who had stayed by our side, recounted an extraordinary and barely believable tale on this subject. "A young man from a distinguished family," said she, "but whose act has made the name unspeakable, came often to the temple, where an evil spirit had made him fall in love with the goddess. As he spent his whole day there, it was first believed to be due to a faith bordering on superstition. In fact he was up way before the dawn, and only went home after sunset, having spent all his time seated before the goddess, his eyes constantly fixed upon her. You could hear him murmuring sweet nothings to her.

16. When he wanted to quench his passion a bit, he would make an invocation, cast on the table four small bones of Libyan gazelle, and read the future in them. If the throw was lucky, especially if it was the one called 'of Aphrodite,' when none of the dice shows the same number, he would prostrate himself, certain his desire would soon be fulfilled. But the opposite was more common, and when the dice were unfavorable he cursed all of Cnidus and, as if his misfortune were incurable, was overwhelmed by sadness. In the

next moment he would gather up the dice and try his fortune again. His passion only grew stronger, and he carved on every wall and tree the name of Aphrodite the Beautiful. He worshiped Praxiteles as equal to Zeus. Any beautiful or valuable thing he found in his house he offered to the goddess; finally, the violence of his desires made him lose his reason, his audacity serving him for pimp. One evening, at sunset, he slid unseen behind the temple door and hid in the darkest corner, holding his breath. The keepers closed the gate as usual, and this new Anchises found himself alone inside. Who would dare recount the sort of deeds he consummated that wicked night? In short, at daybreak this sign of his amorous embraces was discovered, a sign which ever since has marked the goddess as a reminder of her suffering. As for the young man, they say he threw himself upon the rocks, or into the sea. In any case he disappeared forever."

17. Before the attendant could make an end to her story Charícles exclaimed, "So! Even made of stone, a woman wants loving. How then if such a beauty came to life? Would not a night with her be worth Zeus' very scepter?" Callicratides replied, smiling, "We don't know yet, Charícles, whether many more such stories lie in store for us once we reach Thespiae." "What do you mean?" asked Charícles. Callicratides answered, not

without reason. "It is claimed," said he, "that this young lover had a whole night to satisfy his passions at his leisure. Yet he dealt with the statue as with a boy, thus proving he was not seeking the woman in front." When other comments along these lines brought tempers to a boil, I said to them, after calming them down, "O very dear friends, if you are going to argue, do it properly, according to the blessed rules of contest. Stop this disorderly and fruitless spat. Let each of you defend his cause in proper fashion. It is not yet time to board. Let's put this moment to good use in the service of enjoyment, exploring these serious matters in a way that combines pleasure and profit. Let's leave this temple since people are starting to crowd in for their devotions, and let us repair to the garden, there to listen and talk to our heart's content. But remember, he who is bested today is never again to reopen this discussion."

18. It seems I had not spoken in vain, for both agreed. We left, I thrilled to have nought to do but listen, they deeply absorbed in thought, as if upon this debate hung in balance an Olympic prize . When we arrived in a suitably shady nook, offering shelter from the heat of the day, I said to them, "Here is a splendid spot. The songs of the cicadas overhead will be our accompaniment." I sat down between the two antagonists like a true judge, the weight of the Athenian Tribunal heavy

on his brow. I had them draw lots to choose the
first speaker. Charícles won, and I bade him
begin his speech at once.

19. He passed his hand over his brow and, after a
moment of silence, began thus: 'O Lady mine, O
Aphrodite, my prayers call upon you to sustain
my plea for this your cause. Every undertaking,
no matter how small, attains perfection if you but
bestow upon it the least measure of your mercy;
but matters of love have special need of you, for
you are after all their natural mother. Come as a
woman to defend women, and grant that men
remain men, as they were born to be. At the very
start of this debate I call as witness of the truth of
my words the primordial Mother, original source
of all creation, by which I mean the sacred nature
of the universe, she who, having been the first to
unite the elements of the world - earth, air, fire
and water - wrought through their mingling all
living creatures. As she knew we were a meld of
perishable stuffs, granted an all too short
existence, she made it so that the death of one
would be the birth of another, and that
procreation would keep in check mortality, so that
one life could send forth another in infinite
succession. Since a thing cannot be born of a
single source, to each species she has granted
the two genders, the male to which she has given
the seed principle, and the female which she has

shaped into a vessel for that seed. She draws them together by means of desire and unites one to the other in accordance with the healthy requirement of necessity, so that, each remaining within its natural bounds, the woman will not pretend improbably to have become a man, nor will the man wax indecently effeminate. It is thus that the unions of men with women have perpetuated to this day the human race, through an undying chain of inheritance, instead of some man claiming the glory of being uniquely the product of another man. Quite the contrary, all honor two names as equally respectable, for all have a mother and at the same time a father.

20. Thus in the beginning, when men lived imbued with feelings worthy of heroes they honored that virtue that makes us akin to the gods; they obeyed the laws fixed by nature and, conjoined with a woman of appropriate age, they became fathers of virtuous children. But little by little the race fell from those heights into the abyss of lust and sought pleasure along new and errant paths. Finally, lechery, overstepping all bounds, transgressed the very laws of nature. Moreover, the man who first eyed his peer as though a woman, could he have helped but resort to tyrannical violence, or else to deceit? Two beings of one sex met in one bed; when they looked at one another they blushed neither at what each did to the other, nor at what each had

suffered to be done to him; sowing their seed (as the saying goes) upon sterile rocks they traded slight delight for great disgrace.

21. Effrontery and tyrannical violence have gone as far as to mutilate nature with a sacrilegious steel, finding, by ripping from males their very manhood, a way to prolong their use. But these unfortunates in order to remain like young boys no longer remain men, and are nothing but an ambiguous enigma of dual gender, not having kept the one they were born to, and not having acquired the one they have attained. This flower of childhood, having thus lingered a while into their youth, wilts into a premature old age. Yes, we still count them boys, who are already old, for they know not real maturity. Thus vile lust, mistress of all evils, contriving ever more shameful pleasures and ready to stoop to any baseness, has slid all the way to that vice which cannot decently be mentioned.

22. If all obeyed the laws given us by Providence, relations with women would satisfy us, and the world would be washed clean of all crime. Animals cannot corrupt anything through depravity, and the law of nature remains unpolluted. Male lions do not get excited over other male lions, and when in their heat, Aphrodite awakens their desires for females. The

bull, master of his herd, mounts the cows; the ram fills all the sheep with his male seed. What else? The boars, do they not cover the sows in their sty? The wolves, do they not mix with she-wolves? In one word, neither the birds who ride the winds, nor the fishes fated to their wet element, nor the animals on land seek dealing with other males, and for them the decrees of Providence remain inviolate. But you, men of over-estimated wisdom, you truly perverted animals, what novel raving drives you to rise up against the laws and commit a double crime? What blind insensibility blankets your souls, to doubly stray from the good road, chasing that which you should flee? If everyone did like you there would be no one left!

23. Socrates' disciples wield truly admirable arguments with which they fool young boys not yet in full possession of their reason, but anyone endowed with a modicum of sense could hardly be swayed by them. They feign love of the soul and, as if ashamed to love the beauty of the body, style themselves "lovers of virtue." Often I had a good laugh over that. How is it, o venerable philosophers, that you dismiss with such disdain that age where one has long since proven one's worth, and whose gray hairs vouch for its virtue? How come your love, so full of wisdom, lunges avidly for the young, whose judgement is not yet fully formed, and who know not which road to

take? Is there some law tainting lack of beauty as
perverse, and decreeing the beautiful as always
good and praiseworthy? Yet, to quote Homer,
that great prophet of truth:

"His looks were wanting,
But a god granted him beauty of speech,
And all were charmed. He speaks sweetly
Yet firmly too, amid the crowd.
Throughout the city he walks like a god."
And elsewhere he also said:

"In your case, wits do not match beauty."
Indeed, prudent Odysseus is favored over
beautiful Nireus.

24. How is it your love does not pursue prudence,
or justice, or the other virtues which upon
occasion crown maturity, and why is the beauty of
the young the only thing to inflame your ardent
passions? Ought one have loved Phaedrus, the
betrayer of Lysias, o Plato? Was it right to love
the virtues of Alcibiades, he who mutilated the
statues of the gods, and revealed the Eleusinian
mysteries between cups of wine? Who would
confess to being his lover when he fled Athens to
make his stand in Decelea and aspire openly to
tyranny? As long as he remained beardless,
according to the divine Plato, he was loved by all,

but as soon as he became a man and his intellect, previously unripe, acquired its full dimension, he was hated by all. Why is that? It is because these men who call "virtue" the beauty of the body put an honorable label on a shameful affection, and are sooner lovers of children than lovers of wisdom. But so as to not seem to recall the famous only to besmirch them I will not speak further of these matters.

25. Let's now descend from these lofty considerations to an examination of your lusts, Callicratídas; I will demonstrate that the use of women is better far than that of boys. To start, I deem enjoyment to be more satisfying the longer it continues. Desire that departs too quickly ends, as they say, before it has begun. Real pleasure lies in that which lasts. Would that it had pleased the gods for stingy Fate to spin long the thread of our life, granting enjoyment of perpetual health with no foothold for grief. Then we would spend our days in feasts and celebrations. But since some nefarious demon has begrudged us such great boons, the sweetest of real pleasures are the lasting ones. And woman, from maidenhood until middle age, before the wrinkles of old age have carved her face, is worthy indeed of commerce with men and, even when her beauty is gone,

"With wiser tongue

Experience speaks,
Than can the young."
26. On the other hand, the one who courts boys
of twenty seems to me a seeker of passive
pleasures, a votary of an ambivalent Aphrodite.
The body of those become men is hard, their
chin, once soft, has become bristly, and their
muscular thighs are soiled by hairs. As for what is
most hidden, I leave that knowledge to you, men
of experience. Any woman's skin, on the other
hand, shines with grace. Her thick locks crown
her head like the purple flower of the hyacinth -
some spill over her back to embellish her
shoulders, others frame the ears and the temples,
curlier than parsley in a field. Her entire body,
devoid of the least hair, has, as has been said,
more brilliance than amber or glass from Sidon.

27. Why not seek, when it comes to desires,
those which are mutual, and which equally satisfy
the one who gives and the one who receives? We
do not like, in truth, to lead a solitary life like the
dumb beasts, but rather, joined by our mutual
feelings, we find our happiness greater and our
pains lighter when shared. Hence the invention of
the communal table, which one brings out to be
the center of a gathering of friends. If we grant
our belly the pleasure it demands, we will not, for
example, drink Thasian wine by ourselves, and
we will not stuff ourselves in solitude with fancy

dishes. Each finds more pleasant that which is shared with another, and we prefer enjoyments which are reciprocal. One unites with a woman in mutual desire; the two partners part equally satisfied one with the other, after having tasted the same delights, unless we are to believe Tiresias, who claimed the pleasure of the woman far surpasses that of the man. I consider therefore that men should value not the selfish pleasure which they aim to take, but the one which they can afford in exchange. Nobody, lest he be mad, could say that to be the case with boys: the lover gets up and leaves after having tasted pleasures to him beyond compare, but his victim begins with pains and tears; even later, when, I am told, his suffering grows less acute, you will never be anything other than a bother to him, because of pleasure he has none. If we can speak more freely, as suits the woodlands of Aphrodite, I will say, Callicratídas, that it is allowed to make use of a woman in the fashion of a boy, the road being open to a double enjoyment, but the male must never lend himself to effeminate delights.

28. That is why, if a woman can satisfy the lover of boys, let him abstain from the latter, or else, if males can conjoin with males, then in the future allow women to love each other. Come, men of the new age, you legislators of strange thrills; after having blazed unfamiliar trails for men's

pleasures, grant women the same license: let them co-mingle as do the males; let a woman, girded with those obscene implements, monstrous toys of sterility, lay with another woman, just as a man with another man. Let those filthy lesbians - a word that only rarely reaches our ears since modesty forbids it - triumph freely. Let our schools for girls be nothing but the domain of Philaenis, dishonored by androgynous loves. And yet would it not be better to see a woman play the man than to see men take on the role of women?'

29. Having uttered these words with fire and conviction, Charícles grew quiet, his gaze still terrible, almost ferocious. He seemed to have made a conjuration to atone for all love of boys. As for me, I glanced at the Athenian with a gentle smile and said, "I had thought, Callicratídas, that I would merely be judging some game, or lark, but here I find myself, due to Charícles' vehemence, referee over a more serious cause. He has grown heated beyond measure, as if on the Areopagus, pleading for a murderer, or a criminal arsonist, or, by Zeus, for an affair of poison. It is time now to make recourse to Athena's help: may the eloquence of Pericles and the tongues of the ten orators marshaled against the Macedonians make your harangue worthy of those declaimed on the Areopagus!"

30. Callicratídas collected his thoughts a moment or two. To the extent I could judge by his expression, he too seemed ready for combat. Finally he began his reply: "If women took part in government meetings, in the courts and in public affairs you would surely be a general, Charícles, or a president, and they would raise bronze statues in the public squares to you. In fact, the wisest among them, were they to speak in favor of their cause, could not have outdone you - neither Telesilla, who fought against the Spartiates and in whose honor, at Argos, Ares is considered one of the gods of women, nor Sappho, that sweet glory of Lesbos, nor Theano, daughter of the wise Pythagoras. It may even be that Pericles defended Aspasia with less eloquence. But if men are now to speak on behalf of women, then let us men speak on behalf of men. And you, Aphrodite, grant me favor, for we too honor Eros, your son!

31. I had thought our argument would remain on friendly footing, but since Charícles in his speech started philosophizing on the topic of women I will readily seize the opportunity to tell him this: only male love is the joint product of virtue and desire. I wish we stood, were such a thing possible, beneath that plane tree that upon a time heard Socrates' speeches - happier tree than the Academy or the Lycaeum - and against which

young Phaedrus leaned, as the holy man, best
beloved of the Graces, tells us. From its
branches, as from those of the talking oak of
Dodona, we might have heard a voice defending
the love of boys, in memory of handsome
Phaedrus. Alas, that cannot be,

"For between us stretch Shady mountains and
the bellowing sea."
We have halted here, strangers in a foreign land,
and Cnidus is the domain of Charícles. But I will
not succumb to fear.

32. Only do you come to my aid divine spirit,
protector of friendship, hierophant of its
mysteries, Eros, not the mischievous child drawn
by the hands of painters, but Him whom the first
principle of the seed made perfect from birth: it is
you, in fact, who formed the universe, until then
shapeless, dark and confused.

Pulling the world as if out of a grave you have
pushed back Chaos which enveloped it and flung
him into the deepest abyss of Tartarus, there
where there truly are "gates of iron and doorsteps
of bronze," so that he may never return from the
prison in which he has been chained. Then,
beating back the night with your dazzling light,
you became the demiurge of all beings, animate
or inanimate. You have inspired in men, by

means of the exalted sentiment of harmony, the noble passions of friendship, so that a soul still innocent and tender, nurtured in the shade of goodwill, will ripen into maturity.

33. Marriage is a remedy devised by the necessity of procreation, but male love alone must rule the heart of a philosopher. Everything fashioned uniquely for luxury is valued far above that which arises from need, and everywhere people prefer the beautiful to the merely useful. As long as men were ignorant and lacked the ease for seeking something better than the fruit of their daily experiences, they deemed themselves content with bare necessities - they had not the time to worry about a better way of life. But once urgent needs were satisfied, the men who followed after, freed from the shackles of necessity, could improve things; the whole gradual development of the sciences and of the arts that we see today is one interesting result. The first men were hardly born before they had to seek a remedy for daily hunger. Caught by these pressing needs, and deprived by poverty of the freedom to pursue refinements, they subsisted on roots and herbs, or above all on the fruits of the oak tree. But shortly thereafter these foods were relegated to the beasts, and the farmer's toil was directed to sowing wheat and oats, which they had noticed grew anew each year; no one is so

mad as to claim the fruit of the oak is tastier than grain.

34. Furthermore, in ancient times did men not cloak themselves in the pelts of flayed animals? Did they not seek refuge from cold in mountain caves or in the hollows of old stumps or in the old trunks of dead trees? But leaving behind little by little these primitive ways, they wove wool, built houses, and imperceptibly the art of these diverse crafts, with time for teacher, produced beautiful lace in place of simple cloth and lofty roofs instead of simple cabins; magnificent stonework was erected and the sad nakedness of the walls was painted in flowery colors. Thus these arts and sciences, once mute and sunk in oblivion, shone bright after their sleep. Each artist handed down to his successor that which he had invented, and successive beneficiaries, each adding to his own heritage, filled out what was lacking.

35. Let us not expect male love from these ancient times; men had to conjoin with women so that the race would not die out for lack of seed. Multifaceted wisdom and the virtuous desires, fueled by love of the beautiful, could only come to light in a century that has left nothing unexplored; thus love of youths has blossomed together with divine philosophy. That's why, Charícles, do not

condemn as evil all which was not invented long ago and, just because commerce with women has an older pedigree than that with boys, do not disdain the latter. Let's remember that the very first discoveries were prompted by need, but those which arose from progress are only the better for it, and worthier of our esteem.

36. I could barely stifle my laughter when I heard Charícles praise the beasts, and the barren wastes of the Scythians - in the heat of the argument he seemed almost sorry to be Greek. Heedless of undermining his own argument, he did not hide his thoughts by speaking in low tones. Quite the contrary, he raised his voice and fairly roared: "Neither lions, nor bears, nor boars love another male, but their desires drive them solely towards their females." What's so amazing about that? What man chooses by dint of reason cannot be attained by animals, blocked from thought by their stupidity. If Prometheus or some other god had endowed them with human reason they would not be living in the desert or the forest and they would not be devouring each other but, like us, they would be building temples, living in houses by the hearth, and subjecting themselves to common laws. Animals are condemned by their own nature to miss out on the Providential gifts afforded by intellect. Is it any wonder that they should be deprived, among other things, of male love? Lions do not love each other, but they

are not philosophers; bears do not love each other, but they have no understanding of the beauty of friendship. Among men, however, wisdom joined with knowledge, having chosen after numerous trials that which it found most beautiful, has decreed that male loves were the most sound.

37. So, Charícles, spare me these lectures more befitting the wanton lives of courtesans. Don't insult our dignity and modesty in such crude terms, and do not make out Divine Eros to be a little fool. Consider, though it is late to educate oneself at your age, consider now, since you have not done so before, that Eros is a double god, who does not always arrive by the same path, and who does not always excite the same desires in our souls. One, I would say, is a ceaseless prankster; no reason governs him; he inhabits the souls of the foolish and from him come the yearnings for women; he is the inspirer of rapes, for he pushes with irresistible force towards that which we crave. But the other Eros - father of the Ogygian age, honest and profoundly sacred vision, the propagator of healthy desires - fills the souls with sweetness. Under the protection of this god we taste pleasure mixed with virtue. As the tragic poet once said, love has two breaths, and two completely different

passions bear the same name. Shame also is a
twofold goddess, simultaneously good and evil:

Shame can good and evil weave alike
And men in warring camps divide.
For the first she can't be praised too highly
From the bottom of our hearts we blame her for
the other.
So it is not at all surprising if, passion taking the
name of virtue, we should call "Eros" both sordid
lust as well as compassionate affection."

38. "Is marriage nothing then," said Charícles,
"and shall we banish the race of women? How
then will men perpetuate themselves?" "I shall
answer with the words of the all-wise Euripides: 'It
will be better, rather than have dealings with
women, to go into the temples and the sacred
places and purchase children in exchange for
gold and silver, so as to assure our posterity.' In
truth, necessity burdens us down under her
heavy yoke, and forces us to obey. If, by dint of
intellect, we choose the beautiful, then on the
other hand let what is useful yield to what is
needful: Let there be women for making children,
but as for the rest, I will have none of it. What
sane man could stand a woman who, from
morning on, bedecks herself with strange
artifices? Her true figure is devoid of beauty, and
she covers up the indecencies of nature with
borrowed ornaments.

39. If we were to see women as they rose from their bed we would consider them uglier than those animals which it is thought ill luck to mention before noontime - the monkeys that is. That is why they lock themselves in and do not wish to be seen by any man. A flock of old and young servants, equal to them in beauty, swarm around them, offering the disagreeable face all sorts of pomades. They do not refresh their mistress after the sloth of sleep with a splash of clear water before moving on to serious concerns; no, they merely lend, by means of their cosmetics, a bit of color to an unpleasant appearance. Just as at public processions, each one has her function: one holds a silver plate, another a pincushion, a mirror, a host of little boxes just like in a drugstore, vases filled with a thousand poisons which hold the secret of whitening teeth, or blackening eyelids.

40. But it is above all the care of the hair that takes the most time. Some, by means of concoctions which make the curls shine brighter than the noonday sun, dye them as if they were wool and turn them blond, making them lose their natural tint; others, imagining themselves more beautiful with black hair, spend on that the wealth of their husbands, and reek of all Arabia. The iron heated over glowing embers will curl even the

most unruly hair, and the forehead, rimmed with curls to the very eyebrows, is only glimpsed through a narrow opening, while behind them their tresses drape magnificently over their shoulders.

41. Next, they put on flower-colored shoes that cut into the flesh and pinch their feet. A veil light as air keeps them from appearing totally naked. All that is hidden by this veil is even more evident than their face; only women with ugly breasts wrap them in a net. Why bother listing here their spendthrift ways? those Eritrean pearls hanging from their earlobes, worth many a talent! those serpents twisted around their wrists and arms - were they were real and not golden! A crown star-studded with Indian gems circles their forehead, rich necklaces hang from their neck; the gold must lower itself even to their feet to wrap what's left showing of their heels - it were better to put their legs in irons. After their whole body, through some kind of witchcraft, has traded in its bastard ugliness for an ersatz beauty, they redden with makeup their shameless cheeks, so as to spruce up their oily skin with a bit of purple.

42. How do they behave, after all these preparations? They promptly leave the house, and all the gods take their side against the husbands: the women have in fact such gods as wretched men do not even know their names.

They are, I believe, Coliades, Genetylides, or that Phrygian goddess whose ceremonies commemorate her unfortunate love for a shepherd. Later they go to unspeakable initiations, to suspicious mysteries that exclude men - I will not reveal any further the corruption of their souls. Upon their return they take interminable baths, then they sit down to sumptuous meals and ply their men with come-ons. When their gluttony has had its fill and they can no longer stuff their mouth they daintily finger the foods brought before them, and talk among themselves about their nights, their multi-colored dreams, and about their beds, filled with such feminine softness that one needs a bath upon rising.

43. That is how the more subdued among them live. But if we look closely at those who are less so, we would curse Prometheus, all the while reciting the imprecations of Menander:

'Is it not good justice, O Prometheus,
To have you chained to the Caucasian rock?
The torch is your only notable gift,
And all the gods hate you, I am sure,
For having made woman, a race impure.
The men marry, alas they wed!
And then begin furtive desires.
Adultery lies down in the nuptial bed,

And poison in the end, and jealous torment:
That is what woman brings to your life.'
Who would seek such boons? Who would enjoy
such a miserable life?

44. It is only fair now to contrast to these foul
women the manly conduct of a boy. Rising early
from his solitary bed he splashes pure water over
his eyes, still veiled by the night's sleep; then he
pins his sacred mantle over his shoulder with a
clasp. "He leaves his father's house with
downcast eyes," not staring at any passers by.
His slaves and tutors are his honorable
entourage, carrying the revered implements of
virtue: not combs with close-set teeth to caress
his hair, nor mirrors where shapes reflect as in a
portrait, but many-leaved writing tablets, or tomes
relating the virtues of olden days or, if bound for
his music master, his melodious lyre.

45. After having well tempered his mind with
philosophical teachings and nourished his soul
with all kinds of knowledge, he develops his body
with noble athletics. He takes an interest in
Thessalian horses and, his youth once tamed, he
makes use of peace to prepare for war, hurling
spears and javelins with a sure hand. Then come
the games of the palestra, glistening with oil,
wrestling in the dust under the searing noonday
sun, his sweat running in rivulets, a quick bath,
then a frugal meal, allowing him shortly to resume

his activities. Anew his tutors return to relate to him the ancient deeds, and engrave into his memory which heroes distinguished themselves by their courage, by their prudence, by their restraint, or by their fairness. After thus pouring upon his soul the dew of these virtues, evening brings his labors to an end. He metes out the tribute demanded by his stomach, and then sleeps surrounded by dreams all the sweeter for that his rest follows the toils of the day.

46. Who would not be the lover of such a youth? Who so blind of sight, or dense of mind? How could one not love him, a Hermes at the palestra, an Apollo with his lyre, as fine a horseman as Castor, manifesting divine virtues in a mortal body. As for me, heavenly gods, may my life eternally be spent seated before such a friend, hearing his gentle voice up close, sharing with him in all things! A lover would wish to see him reach, after joyful years, an old age free of ills, without ever having felt the spite of Fate. But if, as is the wont of human nature, he is struck by sickness, I will ail with him; and should he put to a stormy sea, I will sail with him; and if a powerful tyrant should cast him in irons, I will be chained with him. Whoever would hate him will be my enemy, and I will love those who would wish him

well. If I were to see bandits or enemies fall upon
him I would take up my weapons and fight
beyond my strength. If he were to die I could not
bear to live, and my last wishes to those, after
him, dearest to me would be these: That one
grave be dug for both of us, and that our bones
be mixed so that none could tell apart our dumb
ashes.

47. Nor is my love for those worthy of it the first
one to be written down: those heroes close to the
gods have thought up this law whereby the love
born of friendship breathes till the moment of
death. Phocis joined Orestes and Pylades
together from infancy; they took a god for witness
of their mutual love, and sailed through life on
one ship. Together they put Clytemnestra to
death, as though both had been sons of
Agamemnon; by both was Aegisthus slain.
Pylades suffered more than Orestes, when the
latter was hounded by the Furies; he stood by his
side when he was accused of being a criminal.
Their loving friendship was not bounded by the
boundaries of Greece, they sailed together to the
farthest shores of Scythia, one ill and the other
nursing him. When they had reached the land of
the Tauri, the Fury, avenger of a mother's death,
welcomed them, and the barbarians attacked
them from all sides at the very moment Orestes
was laid low by his mad ravings, "But Pylades
wiped away the foam and tended him, covering

him with a well-woven robe," showing not so much the tenderness of a lover as that of a father. When it was decided that one would remain behind to be sacrificed while the other was to journey to Mycenae to deliver the letter, each wanted to remain to spare the other, deeming he would live on in the one to survive. Orestes refused the letter, as if Pylades was worthier of carrying it, and was the beloved and not the lover: "If he were to die I could not bear the torment, for my ship is already overburdened with misery." And later he says: "...Give him the letter. He will go to Argos as you have wished, and as for me, let me die as you see fit."

48. That's how things stand. When an honest love, nourished from childhood, gathers strength and reaches the manly age of reason, then he whom we have long loved is able to return that love. It is hard to tell who is whose lover; just like in a mirror, the tenderness of the lover is reflected by that of the beloved. Why ever do you reproach us with a lust alien to human life, when it is one decreed by divine law, and handed down from one generation to another? That which we have received with joy we cherish as sacred treasure. Truly happy is he, as the wise have justly said, who has:

"Young boys and strong-hooved horses!

Joyfully ages the old man
Whom youths do love."
The precepts of Socrates, that admirable judge of
virtue, were sanctified by the Delphic tripod. The
Sybil spoke sooth when she said: "Of all men,
Socrates is the wisest..." Besides all the
teachings by which he benefitted the human race,
did he not teach us that there is nothing better
than the love of boys?

49. There is no doubt that we must love boys the
same way in which Socrates loved Alcibiades,
who slept with him under one cloak the sleep of a
father. As for me, I will end this speech with a bit
of advice useful for all, taken from these verses of
Callimachus:

"You who upon youths cast your longing eyes,
The sage of Erchius bids you be lovers of boys.
Love then the young, the city with upstanding
men to fill."
But know this, young lovers, if you would be wise:
have dealings only with virtuous boys: Do not
barter a long term devotion for a cheap thrill,
otherwise your love will in short order be nothing
but a lie. If, on the other hand, you worship divine
Eros, your beloved's sentiment will remain
constant from childhood until old age. Those who
love in this fashion live delightful lives, their
conscience unstained by anything shameful, and
after death their glory spreads their renown to all

men. If one is to believe the children of philosophers, the heavens receive, after their departure from this world, those who gave themselves over to this love: they go towards a better life, enjoying that immortality which is the reward of virtue.'

50. After Callicratídas had thus spoken, with a certain gravity and at the same time filled with youthful elan, I stopped Charícles, who was about to reply, and pointed out that it was time to go down to the ship. They however pressed me to pass judgement. I reflected briefly on their speeches, and then said, "You do not seem, my friends, to have spoken thoughtlessly or idly; by Zeus, your words are proof of lengthy and profound thought. You have left hardly anything for another to use of what needs be said on this topic, and your eloquence was equal to your knowledge; that is why I wish I were Theramenes the Buskin , so that you could both remain on equal footing, winners both. But since you will not spare me, and also since I wish the rest of our trip to not be troubled by such debates, I will tell you what, at this point, seems the most fair.

51. Marriage is a useful thing for men, and a happy one, if one makes a good match. But I believe that boyish loves, to the extent they obey the chaste laws of friendship, are the only ones

worthy of philosophy. Therefore all should be compelled to marry, but let only philosophers be permitted the love of boys. In truth, virtue does not reach perfection among women. So do not be angry, Charícles, if Corinth yields to Athens.

52. Having pronounced this verdict in spare and subdued terms I rose to my feet. Charícles hung his head like a man condemned to death. But the Athenian, his brow held high, stepped forward joyfully. He looked as if he had just defeated the Persians in the bay of Salamis. I received from him the reward for my decision, for he invited us to a splendid triumphal feast; he was truly quite magnificent in his style of life. I quietly consoled Charícles, praising the force of his eloquence, and I told him I admired him all the more for having defended the weaker cause.

53. Thus ended our stay in Cnidus and our conversation by the temple of the goddess, which mixed playfulness with erudition. But you, Theomnestus, who have evoked these old remembrances of mine, what would have been your decision, had you been appointed judge?

Theomnestus:
In the name of the gods, do you think me such a fool as Melitides or Coroebus to render an opinion contrary to yours? Through my great enjoyment of your words I felt I was in Cnidus

myself, and I almost took this little house to be
the temple of Aphrodite. Nevertheless - since one
is allowed to say anything on a holiday, and the
merriment, even if excessive, is a part of it - I was
somewhat surprised at the pretentious
seriousness of the discussion on the love of boys.
In fact, it seems to me hardly pleasant to pass all
your days in the company of a boy already past
puberty, bearing the torments of Tantalus and
suffering from thirst, his beauty bathing your eyes
yet you unable to drink of it. It is not enough to
see the one you love, to remain seated before
him, nor to just listen to him talk. Pleasure to Eros
is like a ladder; the first step is sight, but as soon
as he has beheld, he desires to get closer and to
touch; and as soon as he has touched with his
fingertips, enjoyment runs through his whole
body. When the occasion presents itself, he risks,
thirdly, a discreet kiss, lips gently touching lips,
and hardly have they met when he draws back, to
quell suspicion. Taking advantage of new
opportunities he indulges in longer embraces; His
mouth draws back time and again, but his hands
must not remain still - daring caresses through
the clothes excite desire. Or perhaps he will
gently slide his furtive right hand into the bosom,
to press nipples that swell a bit more than usual;
he then slowly explores the whole expanse of a
firm stomach, then the flower of puberty in its
early down.

"But why must I spell this out?"
Finally, Eros, having attained the power, goes
about a warmer business and, leaping from the
thighs, as the comic poet says, "strikes where he
must."

54. That, in my opinion, is how one should love
boys. May these sublime sayers of nothings and
all those who aspire to highbrow philosophy
nourish the ignorant with the ringing sound of
honest words. Socrates was a true lover, if ever
there was one, and Alcibiades who lay down
under the same tunic with him did not get up
unstruck. Do not be surprised: Patroclus in fact,
was not loved by Achilles just because he was
seated before him,

"...the holy commerce of your thighs my tears do
mourn..."

I also believe that those whom the Greeks call
"comastes " are none other than professional
lovers. Some might call this a shameful thing to
say, but at least it is the truth, by the Aphrodite of
Cnidus!

Lycinus: I will not allow you, my dear
Theomnestus, to lay the foundation for a third
speech, only the beginning of which would I be
able to hear this holiday - the rest remaining far

from my ears. Let us not tarry any further, and let's get to the marketplace: The pyre of Hercules is about to be put to the torch. The show is not devoid of interest, and brings to mind his sufferings on Oeta.

CITATION: Lucian (or Psuedo Lucian), World History of Male Love, "Eternal Debate", Erotes (Amores), 2000 <http://www.gay-art-history.org/gay-history/gay-literature/homosexuality-debate/lucian-erotes-homosexuality-debate/lucian-samosata-erotes-homosexuality.html

Icon Empire Press

Other books by Robert Joseph Greene:

Visit our website: www.gaybooks.info

This High School Has Closets
(ISBN 9781927124048)

Sometimes coming out during high school just isn't an option. For Mark Thomas, finding out that he was gay falling in love, and dealing with becoming an adult, made it even tougher. High school is a challenge. "This High School Has Closets" is a story of two young teenagers falling in love during a difficult senior year.

The Gay Icon Classics Of The World by (ISBN 9780986929755)

A wonderful collection of gay short fiction fables from around the world. The creation of these stories were based upon some cultural awareness of gay men in history and in some cultures where gay life is taboo. This is a must read for people who are interested in gaining an understanding of gays from different cultures and the human heart. Table of Contents 1. Introduction 2. The Journey and the Jewels – Saudi Arabia 3. And Cupid Also Loved – Rome 4. Haakon of Hearts – Sweden 5. The Wrong Voice Far Away – Egypt 6. Bantu's Song and the Soiled Loin Cloth – Côte d'Ivoire 7. The Five Bows of Shakespeare's Apprentice – Great Britain 8. The Three Wishes – Mexico 9. The Barton – France 10. The Love of Falleron and Ibsen – Greece 11. Halo's Golden Circle – Judea (Israel)

CROSSOVER II: Straight Men – Gay Encounters
(ISBN 9781468072341)

This is the expanded print book from the successful eBook which addresses the psychological struggle men go through in dealing with their desire or curiosity with same sex encounters. CROSSOVER II: Straight Men – Gay Encounters is a collection of short stories that shows what it's like before, during and after such encounters occur.